This book belongs to:

....

Lucy lives at
64 Zoo Lane,
right next door to
the zoo. Every night,
she climbs out of
her window, slides
down the long long
neck of Georgina the
Giraffe and listens to
one of the animals
tell her a story. . .

...and tonight it's the

To Niamh and Felix
A.V.

JOEY THE KANGAROO
written and illustrated by An Vrombaut
Book based on 'The Story of Joey the Kangaroo'
of the TV series 64 Zoo Lane
written by An Vrombaut and John Grace.
The 64 Zoo Lane song: lyrics by An Vrombaut,
music by Rowland Lee, published by Millimages S.A.

First published in 2003
This paperback edition published in 2013

Hodder Children's Books
338 Euston Road
London NW1 3BH
Hodder Children's Books Australia
Level 17/207 Kent Street
Sydney, NSW 2000

A catalogue record of this book is available
from the British Library.

ISBN: 978 1 444 91300 2
10 9 8 7 6 5 4 3 2 1

Printed in China

Hodder Children's Books is a division of
Hachette Children's Books.
An Hachette UK Company
www.hachette.co.uk

tory of

Joey the Kangaroo

An Vrombaut

Hodder
Children's
Books

A division of Hachette Children's Books

In Australia, in the shadow of the Great Red Rock, lived a little kangaroo called Joey. He was too small to jump by himself, but Joey didn't mind. Mum's pouch was safe and comfy . . . just right for a baby kangaroo!

Weeks and months passed by.
Then came spring, and all over Australia
little kangaroos were learning to jump.

'We're practising for the Junior Jump!' said Jimmy
while he bounced up and down.
'I bet you can't jump as high as me!'

Joey tried...

But...PLOOF! He fell down in the dust.
'Joey's got flat feet!' Jimmy laughed.

All the little roos joined in singing:

'JOEY CA-AN'T JU-UMP!
JOEY CA-AN'T JU-UMP!'

Joey walked home, dragging his feet in the sand.

His dad was waiting for him. 'Look, son!' he said and made a mighty leap. 'Now, show me you can jump like your dad!'

Joey tried and tried, but he couldn't lift his feet off the ground.

Then...

PLOOF!

Joey fell down again.

'Blundering boomerangs!' groaned Joey's dad.
'I've never seen a kangaroo who can't jump!'

When night fell, Joey slipped away
to the billabong. He sat on a rock,
feeling sad and lonely.

Plip, plop, plip, plop. . .

Joey's teardrops fell into the water.

'Oh my, oh my, I'm getting a bit wet
down here!' gurgled a voice from the billabong.
'The rainy season has come early!'

And then. . .
RIBIT!
. . .out jumped a frog.

'What's the matter, little roo?'
asked the frog, when he saw Joey.
'I can't jump,' sobbed Joey.
'No worries!' croaked Ribit.

He plunged back into the billabong
and fished out a pair of yellow boots.

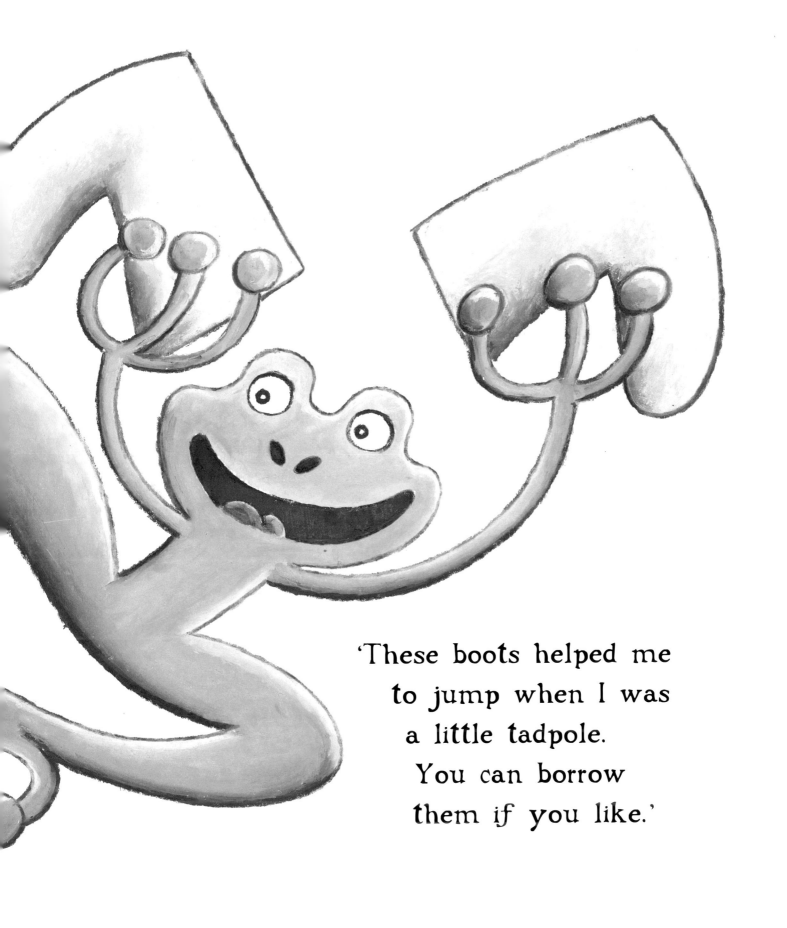

'These boots helped me
to jump when I was
a little tadpole.
You can borrow
them if you like.'

Joey tried on Ribit's
jumping boots.
He closed his eyes.
At first nothing happened,
but then he felt a tickle in his feet.
A tickle that made him jump up!
'I DID IT!' cheered Joey.
All night he practised with Ribit,
jumping higher and
higher and higher!

And when the sun rose
over the Great Red Rock,
it was the day of the Junior Jump.
All the little roos had come to the
billabong with their mums and dads,
grannies, grandads, aunties and uncles.

'Let the competition begin!'

said Mr Platypus.

The little roos took turns to jump over a stick.
Jimmy did a triple backward
upside-down jump.

Then it was Joey's turn.

He jumped up...and up...and up...

...higher than ALL the other little roos!

'HOORAY!'

cheered Joey's mum and dad.

But Jimmy pointed at Joey's boots.
'Hey, that's not fair!' he said.
'Joey's wearing special boots.'

'You're right,' said Mr Platypus.
'Sorry Joey, jumping boots are not allowed.
You'll have to jump without them.'

Joey was scared. He wasn't sure he could do it.

'No worries,' whispered Ribit. 'Those boots are beginner's boots. You don't need them anymore!'

So Joey kicked off the boots. He took a deep breath and started to bounce.

Up and down...up and down...up and down...

Joey could feel the tickle in his feet
getting stronger
and stronger
and stronger...

Until he jumped over the stick and up into the sky!

'The winner of the Junior Jump is. . .
Joey!' announced Mr Platypus.

Joey's mum and dad were
so proud they leapt for joy.
Everyone joined in, skipping
and hopping and bouncing. . .

Even Jimmy – because he could feel
a tickle in his feet too!

Enter the wonderful world of
64 Zoo Lane with these six classic stories:

978 1 444 91299 9

Georgina the Giraffe

An Vrombaut

978 1 444 91298 2

Kevin the Crocodile

An Vrombaut

978 1 444 91301 9

978 1 444 91300 2

978 1 444 91302 6

978 1 444 91303 3